The Adventures of Dandylion and Coppersmith

The Adventures of Dandylion and Coppersmith

Danger, Rescue, and Friendship

John Blevins
Illustrated by Kaylee McCoy

ABUNDANT HARVEST
PUBLISHING

The Adventures of Dandylion and Coppersmith: Danger, Rescue, and Friendship
Text copyright © 2021 by John Blevins
Illustrations copyright © 2021 by Kaylee McCoy

ALL RIGHTS RESERVED
No portion of this book may be reproduced, stored in any retrieval system, or transmitted in any form or by any means, electronic, mechanical, photocopy, recording or otherwise, without the express written consent of the author.

Editing/Formatting: McKenna Hafner/Erik V. Sahakian
Cover Design/Layout: Andrew Enos

Library of Congress Control Number: 2021901489

ISBN 978-1-7349949-6-4
First Printing: February 2021

FOR INFORMATION CONTACT:

Abundant Harvest Publishing
35145 Oak Glen Rd
Yucaipa, CA 92399
www.abundantharvestpublishing.com

Printed in the United States of America

For my grandchildren

Taylor, Kayla, Cahlan, Aiden, Ruby, Zeke, Traeger, Ziylah, and Chezeq

Contents

1. A Son! ……………..……………………………………....11
2. Meet Coppersmith ……………………………….19
3. One Step Too Far ………………………………...29
4. Mother is Not Going to Like This ……………….35
5. Safe for the Moment …………………………….43
6. The Meeting …………………………………….…...49
7. Homeward Bound ……………………………….…..57

Every story must have a beginning!

Count down with me as we begin an adventure of two unlikely friends who come to find that life is a journey, friendship is a treasure, and best friends can face any obstacle this life has to offer.

Are you ready?

10

9

8

7

6

5

4

3

2

And…

Chapter 1: A Son!

He sat on a ledge overlooking his kingdom, the jungle. From the rocky edge he could see the whole valley over which he cared for the animals, both great and small, as did his father and his father's father, farther back then he could remember.

It was quiet today, more so than usual. The animals knew it. Anticipation gripped the whole jungle as they waited. Birds were silent, monkeys ceased their chattering, and zebras their antics.

All eyes were on the King. He sat watching, as if something was on his mind. Waiting…waiting…

"It's a boy!" The young lions cried out. "All hail the young Prince!"

The monkeys went immediately to the trees, taking the news to the jungle. The elephants trumpeted with joy. The hyenas laughed, running into the fields to tell the other animals. And the birds…oh, how they sang, filling the air with songs of the newborn Prince!

Within minutes the jungle burst into life. You see, everyone loved the King. As far back as anyone could remember, the King had always taken care of them …protected them… been fair in judgment. Now he would have a son to follow in his footsteps.

"A son?" The King heard all the commotion and began to smile. "I have a son!" He roared to the valley below, as loud as he had ever roared before. "I have a son," he cried again and again.

The whole jungle heard the King's happy cries and rejoiced with him as he turned to go to his wife and son.

As he neared home, he noticed some unusual looks… And other animals were whispering…

Well, no time for that now. He had to get home. It was a comfortable grassy spot surrounded by trees and a nearby stream. As he came up, all the other animals were huddled around his wife. When they saw the King, they immediately parted and created an opening for him.

With sharp eyes, he looked through the crowd until he saw his wife smiling at him. Then, there was a tiny movement…his son!

The animals bowed low in the King's presence. He walked forward and bent down to sniff the furry little ball cuddled in his wife's lap. "My son," the King whispered in his ear, "I am your father, the King. I am so proud of

you this day."

Suddenly, moved with emotion, the King's eyes began welling with tears and he roared as if he was speaking to the whole world, "This is my son! In whom I am well pleased!"

Even still, the whispering from other animals continued…

"Is everything all right?" The King asked his wife. She gave him a long, thoughtful look.

"Yes," she said. "Everything is fine. You have a son, and I know he will be big and strong like his father." The other animals nodded their heads in agreement.

The Queen continued, "There is one small difference that could possibly affect his later years, but it is of no concern to…"

The King interrupted his wife, not out of disrespect but because the look on her face told him something was wrong. He remembered the whispering he had heard on his way home. "What is it?" asked the King as he looked at the newborn cub. "Two eyes, a nose, a mouth… what could possibly be wrong?"

Suddenly, his son changed position in his mother's lap. The King looked again. He stared. He blinked his eyes and continued to stare.

A tail! Where was his tail? The young lion was missing his tail!

"He has no tail," said the King. He looked more closely. Yes, there was part of one, but it was barely visible. It was more like a tiny stub. The King's mind began to race as he wondered how this could be. No lion had ever been born without a tail! It was something you never thought about because it had never happened before. The Queen sat intently, watching her husband and wondering what he would say or do. The whispering continued around them.

Suddenly, the King stood up and roared, "Enough! Tail or no tail," he sternly said, "this is my son and your Prince!"

Then, looking back at his son, he said in a gentler voice, "To me, you are perfect! You will grow up to be a dandy lion and King."

The Queen smiled at her husband's reaction. She knew the power of love... and the animals began to spread the word.

The new Prince's name was Dandylion.

Dandylion grew into quite a big, long, lanky, handsome Prince. However, he was somewhat clumsy and constantly bumped into things. All the other animals figured it was due to him having no tail, which big cats used to help balance themselves. Even so, Dandylion was loved by all the jungle inhabitants.

There was one problem. It was certainly a trivial matter, and his father assumed he would outgrow it. But as time went on, it appeared that the Prince's "little problem" was getting worse. Dandylion was big and strong, but he was afraid of something. Actually, it was a lot of things! A lot of *little* things!

Bugs, spiders, and even mice terrified Dandylion. The Queen, his mother, was constantly having to save his life from little things.

Also, Dandylion never opened his eyes very wide. He always seemed to be squinting.

"Look at me when I'm showing you something, Dandylion," the King would growl at him.

All the animals had to constantly shout at him, "Dandylion, watch out!" But it was usually too late by the time he heard them. Whatever it happened to be, Dandylion would step into something, fall down, or break something.

"Sorry," Dandylion would say. "I guess I just didn't see it."

Dandylion's problems didn't seem to be getting any better. Still, they didn't keep Dandylion from having fun. The jungle was his backyard and he enjoyed it as often as he could get away. Often, his little adventures took him farther and farther from home.

Chapter 2: Meet Coppersmith

Meanwhile, thousands of miles away in a little English village, there lived a coppersmith. He was a man who used metal to make things like pots and pans. In his cottage there lived a family of mice.

In a small hole in the wall right next to the fireplace, a young mouse named Coppersmith was seated at the little table doing his studies. His parents named him Coppersmith after the cottage owner's trade.

Papa and Mama Mouse did not allow Coppersmith to play with the other mice until his homework was complete. Education was a priority in Coppersmith's home. The problem was that Coppersmith loved studying so much that his parents almost had to make him go outside and play. He loved to ask questions and listened intently to their answers. He even liked homework!

Imagine such a thing…

Coppersmith was a happy and optimistic mouse, quick to find the good in any situation and ready to help others. He was quick to solve problems and liked finding solutions to seemingly hopeless situations.

Often, Coppersmith's family would sit at the dinner

table and laugh at his stories of school and neighborhood friends. The very next moment, Coppersmith would challenge his father, also quite educated, to a riddle he couldn't figure out or a question he couldn't answer.

His father would smile and say, "Well, young Coppersmith, you have me stuck for the moment. I shall think on this for a few days and get back to you."

Coppersmith would always smile with delight and look forward to his father's reply. He could count on it.

Coppersmith had one small problem, though to him it was no problem at all. He found himself often saying, "I couldn't care less." He actually seemed to enjoy the highly polished eyepatch his father had made him to cover his left eye that he lost by staring at the cottage owner's cat one second longer than he should have.

It was a harrowing lesson for Coppersmith to learn and it would have been disastrous had his father not been there to pull him back into their mouse hole. It was, of course, the cat's job to rid the house of rodents and various unwanted creatures. By now, though, all the lizards, spiders, and other small animals had learned to keep out of sight of the cat. It helped that the cat was well fed and getting much slower and a little bigger.

In Coppersmith's enthusiastic way he would say, "I see much more clearly now with one eye than I ever did with two!"

And he meant it!

Coppersmith also had a problem with books. He enjoyed reading them so much that he constantly lost track of time. He was late for everything, unlike his meticulous parents. They tried to give him an alarm clock, they'd set timers for him, and they even asked the rooster next door for help. Nothing seemed to work!

When Coppersmith began to read he was transported to a different place. He could feel, smell, and taste whatever and wherever the book was taking him.

Oh, if only I could see these things for myself, Coppersmith thought. He would wake from his book abruptly when Mama or Papa Mouse pulled his tail or pinched his ear to get his attention.

"Son," they would say, "you're not paying attention again! Go and do what we've asked you to do."

Coppersmith would smile and ask what that might be. Even still, his mother would smile as her quirky son scurried off to do his chores.

Some said it was Coppersmith's personality. Others

said it was his education. Still others said it was simply amazing that Coppersmith wasn't afraid of anything. It wasn't that he was foolish…not at all! He simply refused to let fear dominate his life.

One day, as he was playing in the playground at school during recess, he heard the words, "Fight! Fight!" He looked around and saw a crowd of mice gathering at the corner of the schoolhouse. He quickly ran over to see if he could help.

There in the corner was a terrified little mouse, shaking fearfully in the shadow of the biggest, meanest mouse in the school. Coppersmith didn't even take time to think about it as he jumped in between the two mice.

"You may leave now," Coppersmith told the poor little mouse that was shaking half to death.

"Wha…what did you say?" The little mouse could barely find the words to reply.

"I said, 'You may leave now,'" Coppersmith repeated. "I'll take over from here." His one eye never left the big, bully mouse.

"Who do you think you are?" the bully asked. "Do you want to get hurt too?"

"Oh, dear no!" replied Coppersmith. His mind was racing as he tried to decide what to do. Then he looked the bully right in the eye and said, "I challenge you here and now to a fight!"

Everyone around them gasped as the bully mouse, quite surprised, put up his fists toward Coppersmith.

"Okay," he said. "Let's go!"

"Oh no," Coppersmith stopped him. "Not with fists. With words! You're not afraid of me, are you?"

"Well, I…uh, I mean…" The big mouse had no idea what to say. "Of course I…I…I'm not afraid of you," he stammered.

Coppersmith smiled and said, "Quick, if you can, spell *hippopotamus*."

The children around them began to giggle.

"Hippopotamus?" the big mouse questioned, clearly confused.

"Yes," said Coppersmith. "Hurry up, please! All these other mice are waiting and we don't want to be late for class!"

The big mouse saw every eye on him. Everyone was waiting for his answer.

"Huh…hmmm…" He cleared his throat to speak. There was a slight quiver in his voice as he began to spell the difficult word, "Uh…H-I-P…" Someone started to laugh as the bully mouse hesitated.

"Quickly," Coppersmith said again. "We're all waiting on you."

The bully tried again but couldn't get past the same first three letters.

A small mouse in the crowd laughed. "He can't spell," she cried out.

The bully mouse was so embarrassed that he turned tail and ran away. As he left, the whole crowd burst into laughter.

Coppersmith was a hero that day, but that meant nothing to him. Instead, he saw the tragedy in not being able to spell or read. He found the big mouse later that day sitting by a stream.

"Did you come to laugh at me again?" asked the big mouse.

"Oh, no," said Coppersmith. "I came to be your friend. I can teach you to read and spell!" Over the next couple of months he did just that and eventually they became friends.

One day, Coppersmith went up to his father while he was working on fixing the kitchen sink. "Papa?"

"Yes, Son?" he replied.

"I want to talk to you about something."

"As you can see, I'm rather busy at the moment. Can it wait until I'm finished?"

"No, Papa, it can't!" said Coppersmith. "I must talk to you now."

Papa Mouse remained motionless for a moment. This was not normal for his son. He knew something was on his mind. Slowly he put down his tools and turned to Coppersmith.

"Very well, Son. Sit down at the table and we'll talk. Do you want some tea?" he asked, because no civilized mouse would ever sit at a table to talk without a cup of tea.

"No, Papa," Coppersmith shook his head. "I haven't the time for that now."

No time for tea? Papa Mouse knew this was serious! "Well," said Papa, "What is it then? What's on your mind?"

Coppersmith looked him straight in the eye and cleared his throat. He opened his mouth, but nothing came out. Oh, no! Coppersmith couldn't believe it. For the first time in his entire life, he was scared.

He tried to calm himself down, but his hands and face were perspiring. Papa Mouse could see how nervous his son was. "What is it, Coppersmith? You can tell me anything…you know that!"

Coppersmith gathered all the courage within himself he could find. It wasn't very much at the moment.

"Papa," he squeaked, "I feel that…um, I mean…I want to, uh…" Papa Mouse waited until his son found the right words. "I feel as though I'm reaching the point that…um…I need to…"

Enough was enough. There was only one way to get it out. Coppersmith took a big breath and blurted out what he was scared to say.

"Papa, I want to leave home!"

Chapter 3: One Step Too Far

On several occasions, the King took his son to the farthest edges of his jungle realm. The King taught him well.

"Listen to the other animals," he said. "The monkeys will warn you. The parrots will guide you. Listen to their wisdom."

The King paused. "Dandylion," he said, "do not cross this river! This is where our jungle domain ends. You have all of this land behind you. You are safe here. Do you understand?"

"Yes, Father," Dandylion replied. "'Do not cross this river,'" he repeated his father's words.

Dandylion looked again at the beautiful blue river as his father turned to leave. *It's so big and peaceful,* Dandylion thought. *It would be so much fun to swim here one day.* Little did he know that day would come sooner than he imagined.

Several days later, Dandylion began an adventure of his own. He left home alone and set out to enjoy a beautiful day in the jungle. Jumping and skipping, he trekked along through the trees.

"Dandylion, turn back!" cried the monkeys from the trees above. "You've gone too far!"

The zebras agreed, "You're a good Prince, but the jungle here is too dangerous for you to be alone. Turn back now!"

"I'm fine," said Dandylion with assurance. "I will go back home in a little while. I'm just having a look around." Dandylion knew the river his father warned him about was just over the next hill. He crept forward.

Suddenly, the flowing blue water lay before him. It was a very hot day. What harm could there be in a short swim? He'd surely head back afterward and would be home by dark. Nobody would ever know!

His father's words came back to him…

"Do not cross this river."

Well, Dandylion had no intention of *crossing* the river. He only wanted to *swim* in the river.

The monkeys were clamoring now. "Dandylion," they shrieked, "Don't go into the river! It's too dangerous! Please turn around. Go back home."

Dandylion stood on the edge of the river, staring at the beautiful, rushing water. All he could think of in that moment was how hot it was outside and how good the cool, fresh water would feel.

He took a small step forward, placing one paw in the water. *Ooooh, this feels so good*, he thought.

His father had told him there were many dangers in the water and beyond, but Dandylion couldn't resist any longer. One more step and he was waist deep. He knew he should turn around and go home, but he was so hot and the water was so cool and his skin was beginning to tingle! The river was captivating; it pulled him farther and farther away from the shore.

Dandylion knew how to swim, but the smaller ponds and lakes where he lived were nowhere near as big as the river. He realized he wasn't as strong as he thought he was. In a single moment, the river's current began to sweep him away.

"Help me, help me!" Dandylion cried out.

The monkeys couldn't do anything to help the poor Prince. All they could do was watch as he was swept farther and farther down the river. Soon enough, he was out of sight. They immediately spread the news to other animals. Eventually, the terrible news would reach the ears of the King and Queen.

Only the parrots were able to stay aloft and keep their eyes on Dandylion. He was still swimming, but he was also becoming very tired.

Very, very tired...

Dandylion was in serious trouble! He couldn't stay up much longer and he knew it.

Suddenly he heard some voices. "Look behind you, Dandylion!" the parrots cried out to him. "There is a big tree behind you. You can make it. Try harder!"

Dandylion turned his head and saw the large trunk of a tree floating behind him. "I see it," he said. "I think I can make it!"

He turned around and swam as hard as he could. With his last bit of strength he stretched out his paw toward the tree trunk and caught it with his claws.

He pulled himself up out of the water on a log, but struggled to keep his balance on the big log as he continued downriver.

He looked up at the parrots and said in a voice barely above a whisper, "Thank you."

The parrots turned around and flew away. They, too, were far from home. Even in the air, there was the possibility of danger. Dandylion now knew what his father meant. He wanted to be home more than anything, but at the moment, he was getting farther away.

The heart wrenching news finally reached the King

and Queen.

"I told him not to go there. I told him!" cried the King as his wife wept at his side. They both tried not to think of the worst, but they also knew how dangerous the river was. Their hope was failing when the parrots flew in and landed on a nearby branch.

"He's safe! He's safe!"

"What?" cried the King.

"Dandylion is safe! We saw him. He'll be okay!"

"Oh, thank goodness," the Queen cried.

"Where is he?" asked the King. He knew his son wasn't out of danger yet.

"He is far, far away," the parrots replied, "but we could see from high in the sky that the river widens and grows shallow. Dandylion will make it. He'll be okay!"

They tried to sound optimistic, but the King knew where the river grew wide. It was many, many days away. Even worse, it was where people lived!

Chapter 4: Mother is Not Going to Like This

"You want to *what*?" asked Papa Mouse in confusion. For a brief moment, the older mouse lost his composure. Then, with a sigh, he said, "I think we will have that tea after all. Give me a moment and we will talk about this."

Coppersmith knew his father would hear his side of the story. He took a deep breath and tried to relax. He had thought this through and was quite prepared to talk about it.

He watched as his father finished making his tea. He set the kettle and two teacups on the table in front of them. After pouring the tea into both cups, he sat down and took a quick sip. "Now then," he said, "explain to me this wanting to leave home and why."

Papa Mouse had known this day would come. He also knew Mama Mouse wouldn't like it.

"Papa," said Coppersmith, "you and Mama have been wonderful to me. You've taught me so much. I can fix anything, figure out anything, and face anything. As much as I love you both, I believe it's time for me to make my own way. I know I can do this!"

Papa Mouse knew that his son was just as smart, if not smarter, than many adult mice he knew. He also knew his son could make it on his own. He just hadn't realized how hard letting go was going to be.

The look on Coppersmith's face was enough. His son was determined. With a tear in his eye, Papa Mouse simply said, "Your mother is not going to like this."

Suddenly, Mama Mouse came scurrying in. She took one look at her husband and son and said, "My goodness! Why the solemn looks?"

Papa Mouse sighed. "Mama, you'd better sit down."

After learning of her son's decision, Mama Mouse began to sob. "But where will you go?" she asked, drying her eyes with her apron to no avail. "What will you do? Where will you live? How will we know you're all right?"

Every question Mama asked left her with more tears.

"Mama, I'll be fine," Coppersmith assured his mother. "Don't carry on so. Please! My plan is to go down to the docks in a couple weeks and see where it takes me! I'll be—"

"Two weeks!" Mama Mouse wailed, and then off she ran to her bedroom, the sounds of her cries growing

louder.

Coppersmith looked at his dad, not knowing what to say.

"She'll be fine, Son," said Papa Mouse. "Just give her a little time. Two weeks is very soon. We have a lot to do to see you off. Let's sit down in the next few days and figure out what you'll need. I'll do what I can to help."

"Oh, Papa," said Coppersmith with a smile, "you're the best."

Papa gave him a long embrace then said, "Now off with you."

As soon as Coppersmith left the room, Papa began to cry.

Two weeks later, the day arrived! Coppersmith's whole family stood out in the yard under the watchful eye of the cottage cat. When the cat had learned that Coppersmith was leaving, he figured one less mouse around the cottage would make him look good. And since he'd just eaten and didn't want to get up, the family of mice were safe where they stood.

Coppersmith said his goodbyes to his brothers and sisters, and then it was time.

"Goodbye Papa! Goodbye Mama!" Coppersmith

said for the last time. With one final hug for Mama Mouse and a handshake for Papa Mouse, Coppersmith turned to leave.

The family stood in the yard crying until Coppersmith was out of sight, then they all gathered around Mama Mouse and walked back inside.

Coppersmith was gone and Papa Mouse began to cry.

As for Coppersmith, he could scarcely contain his joy. He was on his own! The small backpack Papa Mouse helped him make proved it. He walked down to the end of the street to an old horse trail. From there he went to the old mill stream. After crossing the small bridge over to the highway, he hitched a ride on the back of a hay truck and took it all the way to the train station. Then Coppersmith rode the caboose to the docks.

Upon arriving at the docks, Coppersmith found himself in disbelief. He saw ships of every size, color, and flag. Men and machines were loading and unloading.

He found a small hole in a large boat container and crawled in for the night. He found a nice warm corner and opened his backpack, fishing out a small cheese and bread dinner. He thought about the day, his family, and what the future would hold. Then he fell asleep.

Clang!

Clink!

Bam!

Coppersmith jumped to his feet, jarred from his deep sleep by loud noises. *I've got to get out of here!* he thought. He quickly gathered his belongings and ran toward the small hole he'd climbed through the night before. He stuck his head out the hole and then immediately stepped back.

"Oh no…"

He was at least 30 feet in the air. A loading crane had set his container high up in a large ship.

"Oh no!" cried Coppersmith, this time louder. He ran back to his corner and waited. "What have I gotten myself into?"

He heard the sound of other containers being loaded next to his. He was afraid of stepping outside until he knew it was safe. After waiting for a while, he heard the sound of a giant motor firing up. Men were calling out to other men. A funny feeling came over Coppersmith and he realized the boat was beginning to move. He stuck his head out the hole just in time to see the large ship moving slowly away from the dock. He could also see a rock harbor and, beyond that, a vast ocean!

Rather than fear, Coppersmith felt delight welling up inside of himself!

"So this is how my journey begins…"

He began to wonder where this ship would take him.

Just then, two sailors walked by Coppersmith's container. The small mouse could hear their conversation.

"How long will this trip take again?"

"We'll be in Africa in two weeks!"

Coppersmith almost squealed. *Africa?* he thought. *How enchanting!*

The ship's name, printed on its side, was the *Santisima Trinidad*.

Chapter 5: Safe for the Moment

Meanwhile, Dandylion's ride on the swift river was coming to an end. What seemed like an eternity later, the river current slowed down and the river widened. Dandylion could see sandbars and shallow areas where he could make it to dry land. He was ready to get off the log, but he wasn't sure where to get off or what to do next. He decided to wait a little longer.

Finally, the log came to rest on a shallow beach. It was only a couple of feet deep, so Dandylion jumped off into the water, walked up the shore, and shook himself off.

Now what do I do? he thought. *I don't know where I am or how to get home.*

He sat down facing the river, hoping his father or someone else would come to rescue him.

He didn't allow the thought to last very long. Deep inside he knew he had drifted very far. Whether he would try to find his way home or continue on, he didn't know, but he knew he had to make a decision. No one else could do it for him.

Suddenly, a movement from behind him caught his eye.

"Who goes-s-s-s there?" asked a large, twenty-foot-long boa constrictor snake. Dandylion was so startled he jumped straight up in the air.

"Excuse me, Great Snake! I mean you no harm, but I'm lost," said Dandylion.

"Los-s-s-s-s-t, are you? I s-s-s-s-saw you come in from the river. Where are you from?"

"My name is Dandylion, and I'm from the realm of the great King many territories from here. I need to get back. Do you know the way, Great Snake?"

"Hmm…I've heard of the great King. S-s-s-s-sorry though, we s-s-s-s-snakes don't move very fas-s-s-s-s-t or very far. This-s-s-s-s is-s-s-s-s my area and I sugges-s-s-s-s-t you leave," said the snake.

"Very well," said Dandylion, "Where do I go?"

"That's-s-s-s-s up to you, young lion, but I'll warn you, this-s-s-s-s is-s-s-s-s not your jungle kingdom. Things-s-s-s-s are much more dangerous-s-s-s-s here. Wherever you go, s-s-s-s-stay off the main trails-s-s-s-s. There are people!" said the snake.

"People?" asked Dandylion. "What are people?"

"Jus-s-s-s-st s-s-s-s-stay off the trails-s-s-s-s-s," said the snake as he slithered away.

Dandylion had to make a decision! He started walking along the river's edge. He walked and walked until he felt as though his legs might fall off.

It was almost dark and he was tired, confused, and hungry. Oh, how he was hungry… Even still, he continued walking. Lucky for him, lions can see very well at night.

A few moments later, he thought he began to smell some food. Oh yes, it was definitely the smell of fresh meat! Dandylion followed the scent to a path that led to a large clearing.

Giant Snake had told him to stay off the path, but it was dark and Dandylion was sure that no one could see him. *I'll be very careful,* he thought.

Unfortunately, Dandylion was much clumsier than he was careful. He started down the path and soon he saw a fresh chunk of meat laying in the middle of the clearing.

Oh, he was hungry!

Oh, it smelled so good!

He took a few more steps toward his dinner and then…

Whooosh!

In a split second, Dandylion was swept off his feet and into the air. He let out a growl so loud that he actually startled himself.

What just happened? Dandylion wondered as he hung in the air, struggling to free himself. He hadn't seen the animal trap in the dark and had stepped right on the trip line. He tried again to free himself but to no avail. He had no choice but to hang in the net until…

Before long, daybreak came. With the morning light came footsteps. Dandylion growled again when he saw them. Even though he had never seen humans before, he understood perfectly. They were hunters and he was the hunted!

Oh, how he longed to be home!

As he wondered why this had to happen to him, he felt something sharp sting his side.

"What was that?" Dandylion cried out in pain.

The tranquilizer dart the hunters had stuck into his fur began to take effect immediately. In a few minutes, Dandylion was sound asleep.

He awoke much later that evening in a crate that was just big enough for him to stand up in. It was made of wood and had a small opening on either side so that he could see out. There was no way of escape.

He continued to look out of his crate and soon he saw the men who had captured him. There were so many of them and they looked so strange. They seemed to be very busy, paying no mind to Dandylion. Through the opening in his box he saw the jungle a long way off in the hills.

He knew he was a long way from home. The feeling that he might never see his home, his parents, or his friends again made Dandylion so forlorn.

Through the opening on the other side of the box, he saw water. Dandylion had never seen a ship before. He couldn't read so the funny-looking letters painted on the ship's side didn't mean anything to him. If he could've read, he would've known it said *Santisima Trinidad.*

Chapter 6: The Meeting

Coppersmith was up early. He was too excited to meet the day to sleep any longer. His two-week trip was finally over! The ship was docked and the sailors had just finished tying large ropes from the ship to the dock.

He was very hungry. The first thing he'd do when he disembarked the ship was find a place to sit and eat a bite from his backpack. He was almost *too* excited, but he calmed himself down, put on his backpack, and scurried down to the deck of the ship. Then he jumped up onto the giant ropes holding the ship in place.

He ran along the rope to the dock and, as quickly as possible, jumped off the dock to dry ground. It felt so good to be on land again!

This is no time to relax, thought Coppersmith. There were too many people moving about.

He looked around and saw a wooden crate off by itself in a field. "Perfect!" said Coppersmith. "Off to the box and breakfast!"

In a flash, he was across the field. He scurried up the edge of the box and took off his backpack. The kitchen on the ship was well-stocked so Coppersmith had lots of food. He opened his backpack and pulled out a small handkerchief. Then he pulled out a small square of cheese and a small piece of bread.

"Oh, how wonderful!" he said loudly.

Before he could take his first bite, he heard a voice.

"Who's out there?" the voice asked.

"Oh my goodness!" Coppersmith jumped to his feet. "I thought I was quite alone. I'm so sorry. I'll leave right away."

"No, please stay," said the voice. "It's good to hear someone else. Who are you?"

"Dear me, I've almost forgotten my manners. My name is Coppersmith and it's a pleasure to meet you. I'm traveling in this land. It's my first day and I am so excited. I was just stopping for breakfast and…oh, there I go again. Sorry! What's *your* name? Would you care to join me for breakfast?"

"Breakfast?" the voice asked. "I'm *so* hungry! I haven't eaten in several days. If you have an extra bite to spare, I'd be so grateful!"

Coppersmith frowned. "I have plenty, but I'm not exactly sure how to get it to you." He looked up and down at the crate. "By the way, what are you doing in there?"

"It's a very long story," the voice sighed. "I almost drowned, got lost far from home, and was captured by men who put me in this box."

"My, my... That *is* terrible. What's your name?"

"My name is Dandylion."

"Well, Dandylion," Coppersmith said, "I think we should get you out of there!"

"Oh, could you? I don't know how to get out. I've tried and tried."

"Let me take a look! I am rather handy at figuring things out!" Coppersmith began walking around the wooden crate. Finally, he called out, "*Aha*! Hinges! That means there's a door back here! There should be a latch around here somewhere..."

Coppersmith climbed up a back corner to the top and found the latch. Fortunately, there was no lock on it.

"Okay, Dandylion. I can open the crate! Are you ready?"

"Am I ever!" exclaimed Dandylion. "Please hurry before something else happens to me."

"Very well," said the mouse. "Here we go!"

Coppersmith grabbed the latch and lifted the handle. With a couple of grunts, the latch slid out of its hole.

"Easy enough! Now, Dandylion, if you'd be so kind as to give this door a kick."

Whooosh!

The rear door flew open. Coppersmith barely had time to grab hold of something to keep from falling.

Coppersmith had absolutely no idea who or what Dandylion was, and Dandylion didn't know anything about Coppersmith.

After a short pause, Coppersmith said, "You can come out now, Dandylion."

The small mouse stood speechless as the large, lanky lion emerged from the narrow cage.

What have I gotten myself into? Coppersmith thought. *Mice do not care for cats as it is, let alone cats that are ten times bigger than normal!*

As Dandylion stepped fully out of the cage, he looked up to thank his rescuer. All Coppersmith could do was stand speechless, motionless, and terrified. What Coppersmith didn't know was that Dandylion himself was afraid of mice. The lion let out a big yell, so Coppersmith did the same.

Oh, what a sight… A mouse with an eyepatch and a lion with no tail screaming at each other in the middle of a field!

"Are you going to eat me?" asked a trembling Coppersmith.

"Of course not! You saved my life," Dandylion answered. "Are you going to bite me?"

"Good gracious no! I just wasn't expecting *you*! I suppose you're free to go now if you'd like. It was very nice meeting you, Dandylion."

"Thank you very much, Coppersmith. You have done me a huge favor. For that I'm in your debt," replied Dandylion.

Suddenly, there was a lot of noise. The men who had captured Dandylion had noticed his escape and were running toward the two animals with tranquilizer guns.

"Run! Run!" Coppersmith yelled. "There's no time to lose! You have to go now!"

"What about you? They may hurt you too!"

"Don't worry about me! Go!"

"No way!" said Dandylion. "Quick! Get on my back and hold on tight as you can! Hurry!"

"But…"

"*Now*!" Dandylion growled.

Coppersmith didn't waste any more time. He jumped up onto Dandylion's back and held on with all of his might. Dandylion picked up Coppersmith's backpack between his teeth and took off running as fast as he could toward the hills…toward the jungle!

And so the adventure of Dandylion and Coppersmith began. They had no idea that they would soon become friends. They had no idea that Coppersmith would soon see the world he'd been dreaming of. They had no idea that Dandylion would one day return home and see his parents again.

All they knew in that moment was that Coppersmith must not let go and Dandylion must run for his life!

The hunters who were chasing them quickly realized that they were no match for the lion and stopped their running. Dandylion, whose eyes were set on the edge of the jungle, was still a long way off and he would not stop until he and his new friend had reached safety.

Coppersmith held on for dear life to Dandylion's mane. He had never gone so fast in his entire life. The men's voices were becoming more and more distant, but Dandylion refused to stop until they were safely back inside the jungle.

Finally, after what seemed like an eternity, Dandylion slowed to a walk. As they walked further into the jungle, the trees got bigger and the bushes thicker! Coppersmith, who was sitting between Dandylion's ears, finally relaxed his grip.

Dandylion came to a halt at last. Several feet in front of him was a small stream…on the other side of it was the jungle! Dandylion took a few big breaths and then, without saying a word, proceeded forward. The shallow stream felt cool to his big feet. He quickly remembered that same feeling was what got him in this sticky situation to begin with. A moment later they were across the stream and stepping into the vast jungle!

Chapter 7: Homeward Bound

No amount of reading could have prepared Coppersmith for what now seemed to engulf him. Trees like he had never seen before in his life created a canopy overhead. They were at least 150 feet high and covered with thick vines! Plants and flowers of every kind seemed to glow in the sun's half-light and shadows. There were beautiful butterflies and moths flying around, all much bigger than Coppersmith himself. Leaves of every size and shape completely covered the ground.

It seemed to Coppersmith that everywhere he looked there was something scurrying or hiding or digging. He could never quite tell what the creatures were, but he knew they could see him. All of a sudden, and without warning, a horrible feeling that he never wanted to return washed over him. Coppersmith was afraid!

Even still, he was speechless as Dandylion continued walking. Coppersmith could hardly take in what he was seeing all around him. Finally, as the jungle began to grow dark from the setting sun, Coppersmith cleared his throat.

"Excuse me…are we going to be all right?" the mouse

asked meekly.

"Of course!" replied Dandylion. "This is where I live!"

Eventually, the two friends came upon a small clearing on the jungle floor. Dandylion looked all around for the most comfortable spot. When he found it, he laid down.

"We'll stay here tonight," Dandylion told Coppersmith. "You'll be safe here with me."

Although somewhat comforted by the lion's words, Coppersmith was still nervous. He was, after all, a mouse, and Dandylion was a very, very large cat.

"Control yourself," Coppersmith said to himself as he gathered up enough courage to finally slide down Dandylion's shoulder to the ground. His one eye opened wide, taking the time to grasp Dandylion's huge size.

Dandylion interrupted Coppersmith's staring. "I owe you a great debt for rescuing me. I can't repay you at the moment, but in the morning I can return you close to where we met. After that I must find my way back home."

"Do you know how to get back to your home?" Coppersmith asked.

"Not exactly…but I'm sure I will eventually."

"Is it far?"

"Yes," Dandylion replied with a frown. "Very far."

"Hmm…" murmured Coppersmith, suggesting he now had something to think about. "Where should I sleep for the night?"

"This is the jungle. It's not a very friendly place sometimes. Just stay close to me."

So Coppersmith took off his backpack and selected a nice, warm, soft spot against Dandylion's chest. Much to the mouse's surprise, he fell asleep instantly.

Coppersmith woke up the next morning cuddled up against Dandylion's neck. After a warm night's sleep, he felt somewhat like himself again, though he was still overwhelmed by all that had happened in the last couple days. He got up off the jungle floor and stretched as the rays of sunlight began to glisten through the jungle's canopy.

There were all sorts of sounds coming from the depths of the jungle, signaling that the morning animals were beginning to wake up. Coppersmith stepped over to his backpack and grabbed a small piece of paper from within. He unfolded the paper, which actually turned out to be quite large.

"You're awake!"

"Oh, dear! Yes!" replied Coppersmith, turning to Dandylion. "I had a wonderful night's sleep. Did you?"

Dandylion nodded his head, but held back from telling Coppersmith that he'd spent most of the night sleeping with one eye open. He knew all too well that nights in the jungle bring another set of dangerous animals. He was on high alert the whole night.

"What are you looking at, Coppersmith?"

Coppersmith smiled. It sounded great to hear someone call him by his name again. "It's a map," he informed Dandylion.

"A map? What's that?"

"Well, my dear Dandylion," Coppersmith said with kindness, "a map is something that helps us know where we are and where we need to go to get you home…with a little study and an ounce of luck, of course!"

"*Home*?" Dandylion jumped up so quickly it startled Coppersmith. "You can help me get home? You would do that for me?"

"Before I fell asleep last night, I thought to myself, this would be something I would enjoy doing! And anyway, it's on my way!" Coppersmith told Dandylion. "I will help get you home and in return, you will help me along *my* way!"

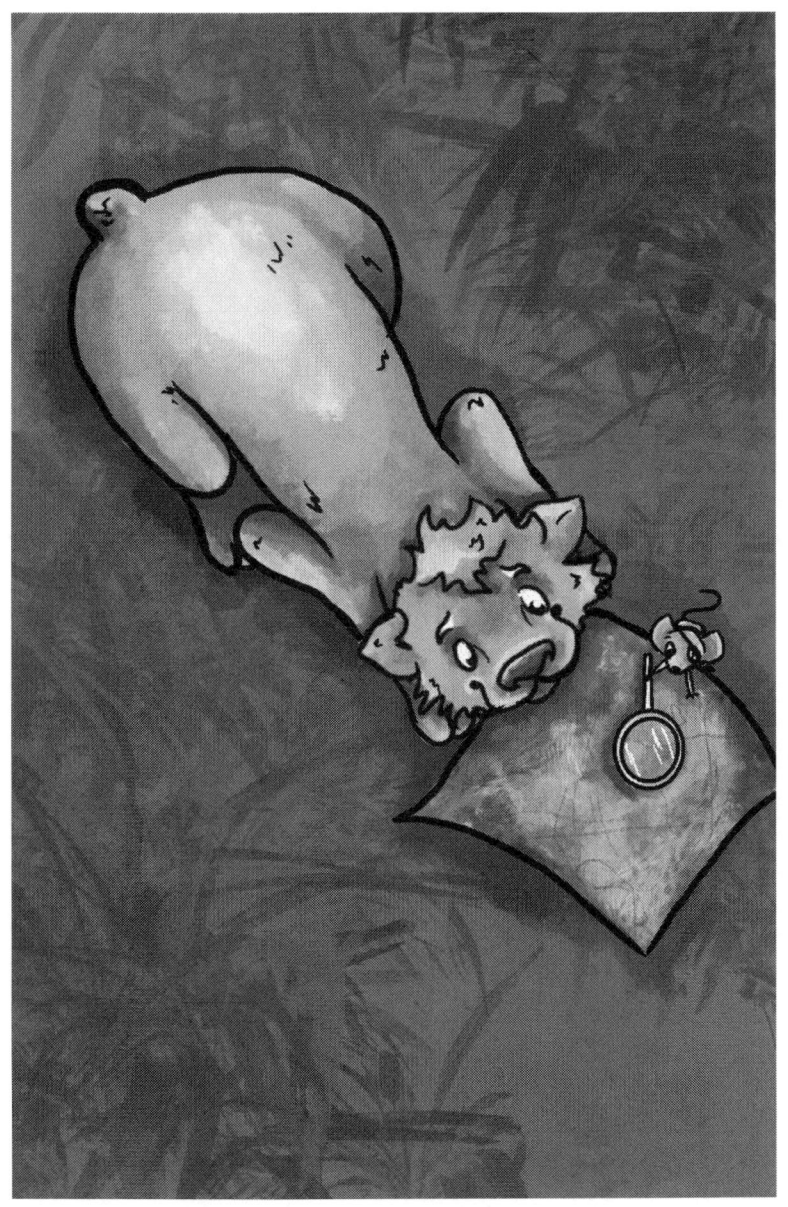

Dandylion let out a roar of excitement, causing the hair on Coppersmith's back to bristle. The mouse put his map away and slid on his backpack.

"Where are you going, Coppersmith?"

"To see the world, my friend…to see the world!"

"But which way do we go?" Dandylion asked.

"Well, let me get my bearings straight," Coppersmith said as he reached back into a small pouch on the side of his backpack. He pulled out a compass and held it up closely to his good eye.

"Wonderful!" cried Coppersmith. "You've already started us in the right direction and soon we will come to another small stream. From there we will follow the stream toward the big river, and before you know it, you'll be home!"

Dandylion was so thrilled that he let out another huge roar as if to say, *Nothing can stop me now! I'm going home!*

Coppersmith quickly covered his ears. "Dear me, Dandylion…you'll have to give me some warning when you roar like that! It's very loud for my small ears!"

"I'm so sorry, Coppersmith! I was just so excited at the thought of being home! I'll try to remember to tell you next time."

Coppersmith smiled as he patted the top of Dandylion's head and got comfortable between the lion's ears. If only his parents could see him now!

As Dandylion walked on, Coppersmith pulled his diary and a pen out of his backpack. He had so much to write about! He smiled to himself as he reflected on all that had happened to him since he left home over two weeks ago. As Coppersmith wrote down every detail, he couldn't help but wonder what was still ahead for him and his newfound friend, Dandylion.

Oh, if they only knew…

A short time later, Coppersmith closed his diary and put it back in his backpack. Immediately his attention turned to what was all around him. Sights, sounds, and smells only added to his excitement as Dandylion continued step by step into the jungle.

Oh, if they only knew…

Acknowledgments

I'd like to give a special thanks to Debbie James and Barbara Black for deciphering my handwriting and putting my words into print, and Susan Chavira for the final redo.

Thank you to my wife and family for their encouragement, and all my grandkids for putting up with my constant storytelling and jokes. Love makes writing a whole lot easier and enjoyable.

Much appreciation to Brittany de Sevilla for first bringing Dandylion and Coppersmith to life.

Thanks to my twin brother, James, for always believing in and supporting my writing.

As always, the greatest thanks to my Lord and Savior, Jesus Christ. May He always be glorified above all else.

About the Author

John Blevins has been a southern California resident for most of his life. Married for 46 years, he and his wife, Debbie, have two sons. John loves spending time with his family who lives nearby.

A veteran of the Army, former pastor, and songwriter, John's many talents have led him to write plays and short stories, and to tell countless tales over dinner to his grandchildren (all nine of them!).

His other passions include spending time in the great outdoors, where he is an avid fisherman and hunter. For 26 years, John has volunteered in his church's prison ministry. He has also written and produced an album of his own original music.

Visit www.johnblevinsbooks.com to learn more.

Made in the USA
Columbia, SC
05 April 2021